Stark County District Library
Lake Community Branch
11955 Mar
Uniontow
330.
www.sta
D0627289
DISCARDED

the Archie® DIGEST LIBRARY

Archie®

– in –

Help Wanted

visit us at
www.abdopublishing.com

Exclusive Spotlight library bound edition published in 2007 by Spotlight, a division of ABDO Publishing Group, Edina, Minnesota. Spotlight produces high quality reinforced library bound editions for schools and libraries. Published by agreement with Archie Comic Publications, Inc.

Library of Congress Cataloging-in-Publication Data

Archie in Help wanted. -- Library bound ed.
p. cm. -- (The Archie digest library)
Revision of issue 176 (Jan. 2001) of Archie digest magazine.
ISBN-13: 978-1-59961-258-4
ISBN-10: 1-59961-258-5
1. Graphic novels. I. Archie digest magazine. 176. II. Title: Help wanted.

PN6728.A72 A68 2007
741.5'973--dc22

2006051170

All Spotlight books are reinforced library binding
and manufactured in the United States of America.

Contents

Archie
Archie
-in-
"WHAT'S IN A NAME?"
HI, POP! WHAT'S NEW?
MORE FAST-FOOD PLACES!
SCRIPT: HAL SMITH PENCILS: BOB BOLLING INKS: JOHN LOWE
COLORS: FRANK GAGLIARDO LETTERS: BILL YOSHIDA
EDITORS: NELSON RIBEIRO & VICTOR GORELICK EDITOR-IN-CHIEF: RICHARD GOLDWATER
I'M AFRAID THE INCREASED COMPETITION WILL EAT INTO MY EATING BUSINESS!
YOU NEED A GIMMICK! YOU SHOULD DO WHAT RESTAURANTS IN HOLLYWOOD DO!
WHAT'S THAT?

NAME SANDWICHES AFTER YOUR BEST CUSTOMERS!
MMM! THAT MAY BE A GOOD IDEA!
I'LL WORK ON THAT TONIGHT!
SHING
CKLE
LATER...
THIS IS REALLY WORKING OUT!
THE NEXT DAY...
HI, POP!
HELLO, ARCHIE! I DID SOME WORK ON YOUR IDEA!
SEE WHAT YOU THINK OF THESE!
2

THE THICK SHAKE WILL BE THE "VERONICA" BECAUSE IT'S SO RICH!...
The Veronica
...AND THE BUTTER-SCOTCH SUNDAE, THE "BETTY" BECAUSE IT'S SO SWEET!
The BETTY
...AND OF COURSE THE "REGGIE" SANDWICH IS...
... ONE HUNDRED PERCENT HAM!
HA! HA!
The REGGIE
100% HAM
THE "MOOSE" WILL HAVE GARLIC AND ONIONS...
THE MOOSE
RIVERDALE
ICE CREAM
POP'S
...BECAUSE IT'S SO STRONG!
3

...I NAMED THE FOUNTAIN SODA AFTER CHUCK BECAUSE...
I "DRAW" SELTZER FROM THE FOUNTAIN!
CHUCK
THE CHOW MEIN SANDWICH WILL BE THE "JUGHEAD"!
THE Jughead
WHY JUGGIE, POP?
BECAUSE AN HOUR AFTER YOU EAT IT YOU'RE HUNGRY AGAIN!
THE Jughead
HA! HA! GOOD ONE, POP!
WHAT ABOUT ME, POP?
I'M STILL WORKING ON THAT ONE!
ARCHIE! WATCH OUT! YOU'RE DRIPPING MUSTARD!
RIVERDA
I'LL MOP IT UP!
4

WATCH OUT!
UH-OH!
I'LL MOP IT UP!
OOOOPS!!
CRASH!
SKIDDDOO
I KNOW WHAT TO NAME AFTER YOU!
THE "SLOPPY JOE"!
THE END

I'VE PROGRAMMED IT TO SHOW HOW YOU'D LOOK WITH DIFFERENT TRENDY HAIRSTYLES!
Archie
-in-
HAIR FLAIR
•GLADIR•COLON•LAPICK•
...THE MOHAWK!
...THE CAESAR!
...THE MULLET!
HOW ABOUT A HAIRSTYLE THAT IMPROVES MY LOOKS?
ONE THAT IMPROVES YOUR LOOKS?
YEAH! YEAH!
NO PROBLEMO!
VOILA... THE COVERUP!
The END

Archie
IN
HELP WANTED
AHA! GOOD TO SEE YOU CRACKING THE BOOKS, SON!
I'VE GOT A TEST COMING UP!
CHIPS
COMPREHENSION OF THE WORLD OF COMPUTERS!
?
POP, I THOUGHT YOU WERE GOING TO HELP ME?
BELIEVE ME...
I AM!
END

Archie in
"GOOF GAFF"
WHAT'S TROUBLING YOU, ARCHIE?
I MADE A BIG GOOF, MR. LODGE!
GULP! I ACCIDENTALLY CRACKED YOUR PRICELESS MING VASE!
TUT! TUT! THAT'S ALL RIGHT! A TRIVIAL MATTER LIKE THAT DOESN'T JUSTIFY YOUR FRETTING ENDLESSLY OVER A---
YOU WHAT?
END

GIVE IT UP, PAL! YOU'RE COMPETING WITH "RABBIT" MANTLE, KING OF THE COURTS!!
HAH! THE ONLY THING RABBIT-LIKE ABOUT YOU IS THE TWITCHY NOSE AND THE LONG EARS!
VOILA! YOU RANK AMATEUR!!
NOT BAD, YOU BABBLING BUNNY!
Archie
in
"DRIBBLE AND DUNK"
-BUT IT WOULDA BEEN BETTER IF YOU MADE THE HOOP!!
PING!

HEY, GUYS! TOSS IT OVER HERE!
HA! DREAM ON, SPINDLE SNOOT!
DON'T CLUTTER UP THE COURT! THIS IS SERIOUS STUFF WE'RE DOIN' HERE!!
WHAT'S SERIOUS ABOUT SHOOTIN' HOOPS?
REGGIE'S RIGHT, JUG! YOU'RE JUST NOT IN OUR CLASS!
COME OFF IT, ARCH!
YOU ACT LIKE IT TAKES SOME KIND OF UNCANNY SKILL!
AND YOU THINK IT DOESN'T? WATCH THIS!
OKAY! MAYBE THAT WASN'T MY BEST EXAMPLE!
I'LL BUY THAT!
PING!
ALL RIGHT, JUGGIE! WHAT'S GOING ON WITH THOSE MAVENS OF MACHONESS?
ANOTHER NEW WORD, RON?
2

I THINK THEY'RE TRYIN' TO SEE WHO CAN SCORE MORE NEAR MISSES!
THERE'S MORE TO IT THAN SHOOTING, WISE GUY!
YOU ALSO GOTTA KNOW HOW TO DRIBBLE!
OH, HE DRIBBLES WITH THE BEST OF THEM!
THUMP! THUMP!
LEARNED IT AS A BABY IN THE HIGH CHAIR!
OH, YES! CUTE, BUT SLOPPY!
HMPH! WISENHEIMERS, TOO!
WELL, WHAT DO YOU SAY? SHALL WE HAVE A GO?
WHY NOT?
HEY! WATCH THAT.!!
WOOSH!
TSK! THEY DON'T WANT TO SHARE, BETTY!
HOW UNFRIENDLY!
FLIP!
3

C'MON! GIVE US BACK OUR BALL!
STOP BEIN' SO POLITE, ARCH!
JUST RUSH IN AND TAKE IT AWAY!
TAKE WHAT AWAY, REGINALD?
LET'S SEE! IS THIS HOW YOU EXPERTS DRIBBLE?
GRRR!
WOOSH!
ZOOM!
SLAP!
EEP!! -- W-WHERE'D HE GO?
SHOOT, BETTY!
TZING!
STREAK!
4

PERFECT!
IS THAT THE WAY TO DO IT, BOYS?
FLIP!
SWISH!
GEE! WITH A LITTLE PRACTICE, WE MIGHT BE AS GOOD AS THEY ARE!
SMACK!
BUMP!
BUMP!
HUMPH! DUMB GAME! I'LL TAKE SOCCER ANYTIME!
RIGHT YOU ARE! SOMETHING WORTHY OF OUR SUPERIOR SKILLS!
END

Archie in "GLAD HAND GURU"
RON, YOU'VE BEEN STARING AT YOUR HAND FOR TEN MINUTES! IS THERE SOMETHING WRONG WITH IT?
AU CONTRAIRE, MY SWEET! IT'S A WONDERFUL HAND... AN OUTSTANDING HAND... A VERY REVEALING HAND!
"REVEALING"?
I'VE BEEN STUDYING PALMISTRY! THE HAND TELLS THE FUTURE!
SHEESH! THAT STUFF IS COMPLETE NONSENSE!
IT IS A SCIENCE! PURE AND SIMPLE!

ESPECIALLY SIMPLE!
YOU'D NEVER GUESS WHAT THAT LOVELY HAND TELLS ME!
HMM! I SEE PAMPERED! I SEE SPOILED! I SEE NO SIGNS OF A CALLOUS! I SEE SERVANTS AND OODLES OF MONEY!
GASP! YOU'VE BEEN STUDYING PALMISTRY!
YOU'RE ABSOLUTELY RIGHT! AND ASIDE FROM THAT, IT SHOWS THAT I AM DESTINED FOR EVEN GREATER GREATNESS!
DARN! HOW DID I MISS THAT?
WHAT GIVES, GIRLS?
RON READS PALMS!
BETTY DOES PRETTY WELL HERSELF!
SHE READ ME LIKE A BOOK! A VERY FINE BOOK, BOUND IN GENUINE, EXPENSIVE LEATHER!
NO PAPER-BACKS IN THAT HAND!
LET ME DO YOURS NOW, BETTY! ARE YOU READY TO HAVE YOUR FUTURE REVEALED?
READY AS I'LL EVER BE!
2

HMM! I SEE GOOD NEWS AND BAD! WHICH DO YOU WANT FIRST?
LET'S GET THE BAD OUT OF THE WAY!
YOU ARE NOT GOING TO BE VERY LUCKY IN LOVE!
ESPECIALLY WITH FRECKLE-FACED RED-HEADS, HUH?
THE GOOD NEWS IS THAT YOU ARE GOING TO DEVOTE YOUR LIFE TO THE PEACE CORPS, HELPING THE UNFORTUNATE!
(SIGH) THAT'S WHAT I HOPED TO DO FOR THE REDHEAD!
AS LONG AS WE'RE PLAYING SILLY GAMES, DO US!
OKAY! GO WASH YOUR HAND, JUGGIE!
SEE THAT LINE? THAT TELLS ME YOU'RE GOING TO MARRY A BEAUTIFUL BRUNETTE!
OH, WOW!
JUST ONE?
WHO KNOWS? SHE MIGHT BE RIGHT IN THIS SCHOOL! I'VE GOT TO FIND HER!
HEY!
3

A BEAUTIFUL BRUNETTE! THAT COULD BE MIDGE!
MOOSE'S GIRL? THAT WOULD NOT BE GOOD LUCK, PAL!
WHAT IN THE WORLD DO YOU THINK THIS IS?
HAIR?
BLACK HAIR ... AS IN BRUNETTE, YOU IDIOT! I WAS TALKING ABOUT ME!!!
OH!
BRRING!
OOPS! THERE'S THE BELL! WE'D BETTER GET TO CLASS!
NEXT DAY...
ANYBODY SEEN BETTY? WE ALWAYS GET TOGETHER ON SATURDAY MORNINGS!
YEAH! I SAW HER! SHE WAS HEADING TOWARD THE BUS STOP, CARRYING A VALISE!
OH, NO!
4

THE PEACE CORPS! SHE'S JOINED THE PEACE CORPS!!
PO
IT'S ALL YOUR FAULT, RON! SHE MUST HAVE BELIEVED THAT GARBAGE YOU WERE HANDING OUT YESTERDAY!
HURRY! WE MUST STOP HER!
10
BETTY! NO! THERE WAS NO TRUTH IN THOSE PALM READINGS I WAS GIVING!!
HECK, I KNEW THAT!
THEN YOU'RE NOT JOINING THE PEACE CORPS?
NOT UNTIL I FINISH HIGH SCHOOL, AT LEAST!
MY DAD'S FAVORITE PIECE OF LUGGAGE! THE HANDLE BROKE! I'M TAKING IT TO GET IT REPAIRED!
WHEW! WHAT A RELIEF!
YES, INDEEDY! LET'S ALL GO HAVE A CUP OF TEA! I'VE LEARNED TO READ TEA LEAVES! MUCH MORE DEPENDABLE THAN PALMS!
MADAME OLGA'S TEA ROOM
10
END

Archie
in
"ANIMAL ANTICS"
VERONICA, YOUR ANIMAL MASQUERADE IS THE GREATEST!
WHERE'S ARCHIE?
I'M MAD AT HIM, ETHEL!
--- I WOULDN'T SPEAK TO HIM EVEN IF HE CAME CRAWLING BACK TO ME!
I THINK HE IS TRYING TO CRAWL BACK TO YOU!
The End

Archie
"TIME'S UP"
UH - OH!
PUFF PUFF
PUFF PUFF
PHEW!
VIOLATION
AA1
END

Archie in "POLLUTION SOLUTION"
HEY, GIRLS!
I'M SURE I CAN GET SOME VOLUNTEERS FOR YOUR RECYCLING SQUAD, COMMISSIONER GREEN! AS PRINCIPAL I ENJOY A CLOSE RELATIONSHIP WITH MY STUDENTS!
??
MR. WEATHERBEE PRINCIPAL
CRASH
I SEE WHAT YOU MEAN, WEATHERBEE!
ARCHIE, INSTEAD OF WATCHING GIRLS, WHY DON'T YOU WATCH WHERE YOU'RE GOING?!
I'LL TRY, SIR...HI, JEN! HI, ANNIE!

ARCHIE!!
I CAN'T HELP IT, MR. WEATHERBEE! YOU KNOW WHAT HAPPENS WHEN I SEE A PRETTY GIRL!
IT MUST BE SOMETHING IN THE AIR THAT MAKES ME FALL IN LOVE WITH EVERY GIRL I SEE!
THEN YOU WON'T MIND IF I VOLUNTEER YOU FOR COMMISSIONER GREEN'S TEEN RECYCLING SQUAD!
ME?
YES! HELPING TO PREVENT AN ECOLOGICAL DISASTER IS A GREAT WAY TO TAKE YOUR MIND OFF GIRLS, ARCHIE!
YES, SIR!
UH... ARE YOU SURE ABOUT THIS, WEATHERBEE?
OF COURSE! I KNOW HOW TO DEAL WITH "LOVE SICKNESS" FROM MY OWN DAYS AS A LAD! WEATHERBEE THE HONEYBEE THEY USED TO CALL ME! HEE! HEE!
THE FOLLOWING SATURDAY...
I NEVER REALIZED THERE WERE SO MANY OLD TIRES IN PEOPLE'S GARAGES, COMMISSIONER!
YOU'RE DOING A GREAT JOB, ARCHIE!
RIVERDALE
EPD
2

JUST TRY NOT TO PILE THESE TIRES TOO HIGH!
I'LL LOWER SOME OF THESE STACKS!
HI, ARCHIE!
ANGELA! I DIDN'T KNOW YOU LIVED AROUND HERE...
211710
WHOOPS!
THUMP THUMP!
RDALE
EPD
OW! OW!
27
COMMISSIONER! ARE YOU OKAY?
SURE, ARCHIE! I'M JUST TIRED!
SOON...
HMPF! NOW HE'S TALKING TO GIRLS INSTEAD OF LOADING NEWSPAPERS!
3

ARCHIE, WILL YOU PLEASE HELP ME LOAD THE REST OF THESE PAPERS ONTO THE TRUCK? ARCHIE?!
HUH?... OH, SURE! LATER, GIRLS!
WHOA! WHAT A GUST OF WIND! I'M GLAD I TOLD YOU TO TIE THE NEWSPAPERS UP BEFORE STACKING THEM!
WOOOOSH!
YOU DID?
!!
HOURS LATER...
STAY IN THE TRUCK, ARCHIE, AND TRY TO KEEP OUT OF TROUBLE...
RIVERDALE RECYCLING PLANT
RIVERDALE
EPD
... UNTIL THE PLANT MANAGER TELLS US WHERE TO UNLOAD THE CANS WE COLLECTED!
I PROMISE NOT TO TALK TO ANY GIRLS, COMMISSIONER!
4

HI! ALL SET TO UNLOAD?
YOU'RE THE PLANT MANAGER?!
I'M READY TO BE RECYCLED... I MEAN, I'M READY TO RECYCLOPEDIA... I MEAN....
CRANK!
WAIT! NOT YET!
RRRRUMBLE!
RIVERDALE EPD
KRASH!
!
DON'T TELL ME...
MONDAY MORNING...
SO WAS MY LITTLE PLAN A SUCCESS?
FORGET YOUR PLAN, WEATHERBEE! WE'VE GOT TO ALERT THE WORLD TO THE WORST ECOLOGICAL DISASTER YET...
...ARCHIE ANDREWS!!
!!
End

Archie's GAG BAG
ARCHIE, DON'T YOU UNDERSTAND THIS FORMULA?
I'M ON THE RIGHT CHANNEL, BUT I HAVEN'T GOT TUNED IN CLEAR!
I HAD THE WHOLE THING ON THE BOARD THIRTY SECONDS AGO!
I GUESS MY VIDEO TUBE LOST THE PICTURE!
WILL YOU GET YOUR MIND OFF TV!
NOW.... WHAT WAS THE FORMULA?
COULD WE HAVE AN INSTANT REPLAY?
END

Archie
IN
"GOOD ADVICE"
OKAY- THE NEXT OPPONENTS WILL BE ARCHIE AND MOOSE.!
COACH, YOU CAN'T PUT ME IN THE RING WITH MOOSE, HE'LL MURDER ME.!
DON'T LET HIS SIZE THROW YOU, ARCHIE.! DAZZLE HIM WITH YOUR FOOTWORK.!
FOOTWORK, EH? OKAY.!
LET ME KNOW WHEN HE'S DAZZLED.!
THE END

GET SET FOR ANOTHER GREAT STORY WITH ME BACK WHEN I WAS KNOWN AS...
Little Archie

Little Archie
"GHOST OF A CHANCE"
AS THE SUN POKED HIS HEAD OVER THE TREES, ALL THE SKELETONS WENT BACK TO THE CEMETERY TO WAIT UNTIL HALLOWEEN NEXT YEAR....
...AND THE GOBLINS WENT BACK INTO THE OLD HAUNTED HOUSE.. ALL EXCEPT ONE!
WHERE (SHIVER) D-DID HE G-GO?
RIGHT HERE!
LOOK! IT WAS LITTLE ARCHIE!
I'M GLAD ALL OF US KNOW GOBLINS AND GHOSTS AREN'T REAL!
ALL OF US EXCEPT EVELYN EVERNEVER!

THAT ENDS THE HALLOWEEN PARTY, KIDS!
OKAY, GOOD NIGHT, LITTLE ARCHIE!
EVERYONE'S GONE EXCEPT YOU, EVELYN!
IT'S KINDA SPOOKY OUT THERE, MR. ANDREWS!
LITTLE ARCHIE AND SPOTTY WILL WALK YOU HOME!
DON'T YOU AND MRS. ANDREWS WANT TO COME?
YOU ONLY LIVE FOUR HOUSES AWAY!
WE'LL LEAVE THE PORCH LIGHT ON!
WHEN IT GETS DARK, I THINK I SEE GHOSTS COMING AFTER ME!
RELAX, EVELYN, NO GHOSTS WILL COME AFTER YOU!
T-THEY WON'T?
NO! 'CAUSE THERE'S NO SUCH THING AS GHOSTS!
2

T-THERE ISN'T?
COURSE NOT! MY FATHER TOLD ME SO THIS AFTERNOON!
T-THEN W-WHY IS THAT GHOST S-SITTING OVER T-THERE?
W-WHERE?
S-SITTING OVER THERE O-ON THAT STUMP!
HUMPH! I DON'T SEE ANYBODY!
IF YOU SEE HIM SO GOOD, WHAT DOES HE LOOK LIKE?
W-WELL, (GULP) H-HE'S WEARING A BIG WHITE SHEET...
... AND A BIG, LONG, POINTED NOSE AND ONE OL' GREEN EYE...
... HORNS COMING OUT HIS HEAD AND...
HOLD IT! EVELYN!
3

IN THE FIRST PLACE, GHOSTS DON'T LOOK LIKE THAT!
NO?
A GHOST WOULD NEVER LOOK THAT SILLY!
OOOH!
NOW YOU'VE GOT HIM MAD!
HE'S GETTING UP AND COMING OVER TO YOU!
.... HIS LONG, BONY FINGERS REACHING OUT...
BUT SUPPOSE THE GHOST COMES AFTER ME?
DON'T WORRY! I'M THE ONE HE'S AFTER!
END

Little Archie
"THE HAUNTED HOUSE ON HALLOWEEN HILL"
HEH! HEH! I HOPE EVERYONE WILL HAVE A GOOD TIME TONIGHT!
WE SURE WILL, MR. WEATHERBEE!
HALLOWEEN IS A FUN TIME FOR EVERYONE!
7
REMEMBER! AFTER WE TRICK-OR-TREAT, WE'LL COME BACK TO SCHOOL FOR REFRESHMENTS AND PICK THE BEST COSTUME!
WHAT'S THE PRIZE?
MAYBE IT'S A KISS FROM BETTY!
GEE! THAT OUGHTA BE THE BOOBY PRIZE!

AW, BETTY CAN'T TAKE AN OLD JOKE.!
YEAH.!--- AND YOU CAN'T TAKE A FEW LEFTS AND RIGHTS, HEH, HEH!
WHAT ARE YOU GOING TO DRESS UP AS TONIGHT, MR. WEATHERBEE ?
IT'S ALWAYS A SECRET, MISS GRUNDY.! BUT IT'S APPROPRIATE FOR HALLOWEEN.! HEH.! HEH.!
MAN.! THE BEE PUTS ON A MANGY MONSTER OUTFIT AND ALL THE KIDS HAVE TO FAKE IT THAT THEY'RE SCARED.!
(YAWN.!) IT'S THE SAME STORY EVERY YEAR.!
AND SO AS HALLOWEEN EVENING COMES, LITTLE ARCHIE AND HIS FRIENDS DRESS UP IN COSTUMES-
I'M GOING OUT AS A TRAMP, DAD.!
OOMPH.! THAT'S ONE OF MY JACKETS.!
NEWS
TRICK OR TREAT
AH, REGGIE.! YOU'RE A HANDSOME DEVIL.!
I HOPE LITTLE ARCHIE LIKES MY COSTUME.!
I LOVE TRICK OR TREATS ---
--MOSTLY TREATS.! SMACK.!
2

WHY DON'T YOU GET WITH IT, JUGGIE? YOU GO OUT AS A HAMBURGER EVERY YEAR!
WRONG, REG! THIS YEAR IT'S DIFFERENT---
--THIS YEAR I PUT IN A BUILT-IN SNACK TRAY!
WOW! YOU EVEN HAVE A PLACE FOR MUSTARD AND KETCHUP!
WE NOW SWITCH TO THE BEE'S HOUSE---
I HOPE I CAN PUT A FEW SCARES INTO THE CHILDREN THIS YEAR, TOO!
Y' KNOW, THERE'S ONLY ONE THING BAD ABOUT WALKING TO SCHOOL!
YEAH! (CHOKE!) YOU HAVE TO PASS BY THE HAUNTED HOUSE!
IT ALWAYS LOOKS SCARY AT NIGHT, TOO!
'SPECIALLY ON HALLOWEEN!
YAAG!
I SEE SOME-THING!
HA! HA! THE ONLY THING YOU EVER SEE BESIDES FOOD ARE SPOOKS!
JUGGIE'S A REAL BELIEVER IN HALLO-WEEN!
3

NO! NO! I SAW A LIGHT IN THE WINDOW!
WELL, IT'S GONE NOW!
C'MON! LET'S MOVE ALONG A LITTLE FASTER!
TREAT
DID JUGHEAD SEE ANYTHING? LET'S TAKE A TERROR-FILLED PEEK INSIDE THE OLD HOUSE --
A-ARE WE READY, DEXTER?
THE FINAL MOMENT IS HERE!
TONIGHT, MY MASTERPIECE COMES TO LIFE!
WOWIE! I THOUGHT HE WAS FLAKY AS A CARTOONIST, BUT HE'S REALLY FLIPPED OUT AS A NUTTY SCIENTIST!
LOOK! THE MONSTER MOVES!
ZZZT
AGGR!
GO! PREY UPON THE PEOPLE OF RIVERDALE!
THIS WILL SHOW EVERYONE WHO LAUGHED AT ME!
TOO BAD THEY DIDN'T LAUGH AT YOUR CARTOONS, HUH, DEX?
4

EGAD! IT'S ALMOST TIME FOR THE PARTY AND I CAN'T FIND MY BOOT---
---I'LL NEVER GET THERE!
AGRR!
HERE COMES THE BEE IN HIS MONSTER SUIT AGAIN!
LET'S GIVE OUT WITH THE SCARED BIT AGAIN!
AGRRR!
EEEE! LOOK AT HIM OPEN THOSE DOORS!
I NEVER KNEW HE WAS THAT STRONG!
HE'S HEADING FOR THE CHOW TABLE!
YEAH! THE BEE LIKES FOOD ALMOST AS MUCH AS JUGGIE!
TAKE IT EASY! ALL THE CHILDREN ARE WATCHING YOU!
YES! YOU'RE MAKING A BIG PIG OF YOURSELF!
H-HE'S FINALLY STOPPING!
THAT'S BECAUSE HE DRANK EVERYTHING!
5

BURP!
OOOH!
IT'S HARD TO RUN ON ONE BARE FOOT!
LOOK AT HIM EAT THE DOUGHNUTS!
OOOH! I'M SO MAD!
LEAVE SOME FOR ME!!
AGR!
WHAM!
BOY! MR. WEATHERBEE'S GOT A REAL TEMPER!
ALL JUGGIE HAS IS THE BEE'S BOOT!
HERE I AM, CHILDREN!
HEY! THE BEE GOES OUT ONE DOOR AND COMES IN ANOTHER!
HOW DOES HE DO THAT?
6

YOU SURE PLAYED THE PART OF A MONSTER TONIGHT, MR. WEATHERBEE.!
YOU PACK A WALLOP, TOO.!
?
HERE'S YOUR BOOT BACK TOO, MR. WEATHERBEE.!
MY WORD.! HOW DID YOU GET IT HERE, JUGHEAD?
HEH.! HEH.! A PERFECT FIT.!
I THINK HALLOWEEN HAS GONE TO HIS HEAD.!
ALL THE KIDS THINK YOUR COSTUME DESERVES FIRST PRIZE, MR. WEATHERBEE.!
CHILDREN, I- I'M SPEECHLESS! (SNIFF.!)
I WONDER WHY THE TEACHERS ARE LOOKING AT ME SO STRANGELY?
(SOB.!) MY MONSTER DOESN'T SCARE ANYONE.!
HE SCARES ME.! WHAT'LL HE DO TO US WHEN WE RUN OUT OF CIDER AND DOUGHNUTS?
THE END

IMPOSSIBLE YOU SAY....? NOT AFTER YOU'VE READ THE STRANGE STORY OF "**THE HOUSE THAT WOULDN'T MOVE....**"

YOUR FATHER'S TRYING TO KEEP A NEW STATE HIGHWAY FROM CUTTING RIVERDALE IN HALF!
CAN'T THE STATE BUILD THE HIGHWAY AROUND RIVERDALE?
THAT'S WHAT YOUR FATHER WANTS! BUT THE MAYOR WILL BENEFIT FROM THE SALE OF SOME OF HIS LAND! HE'S TALKED THE STATE COUNCIL INTO BRINGING THE ROAD RIGHT THROUGH TOWN!
AW, DAD WILL MAKE 'EM CHANGE THEIR MINDS!
I DON'T KNOW! A WRECKING CREW WILL START TEARING DOWN THE OLD COLLINS PLACE TOMORROW!
THE HAUNTED HOUSE ON THE HILL!
THE HIGHWAY IS GOING TO BE THERE! BETTER TAKE A LAST LOOK AT THE PLACE!
GEE, BETTY! I THINK WE SHOULD TAKE A LAST WALK THROUGH THE OL' PLACE!
ULP! THROUGH THAT?
2.

BESIDES, HEH! HEH! THIS IS OUR LAST CHANCE TO BE **SCARED!**
WONDER WHAT THIS OL' HOUSE WOULD SAY IF IT KNEW IT WASN'T GOING TO BE HERE TOMORROW?
Z Z Z Z
BETTY, WAIT! THE SOUND'S COMING FROM THIS ROOM!
Z Z Z Z Z Z Z Z Z
3

L-LET'S GET OUT OF HERE!
HOLD UP THERE! WHERE DO YOU THINK YOU'RE RETREATING TO?
CONFOUND IT, CHILDREN! PUT YOUR EYEBALLS BACK IN YOUR HEAD!
I-I'M SORRY, SIR, B-BUT THIS IS T-THE FIRST TIME W-WE'VE EVER SEEN A G-GHOST!
WELL, USUALLY I SLEEP IN THE CELLAR DAYTIMES AND COME UP TO HAUNT JUST AT NIGHT!
LATELY I'VE BEEN PUTTING IN A LOT OF NIGHT TIME DUTY... I GOT EXTRA TIRED AND FELL ASLEEP RIGHT HERE!
BETTER FIND ANOTHER PLACE TO SLEEP, SIR! THEY'RE TEARING DOWN THIS HOUSE TOMORROW!
WHAT'S THAT?
A NEW STATE HIGHWAY IS GOING OVER THIS VERY SPOT!
4

NOSSIRREEE! THIS HOUSE IS GOING TO STAND A FEW MORE YEARS OR MY NAME ISN'T GENERAL COLLINS!
Y-YOU'RE GENERAL COLLINS!
THAT I AM, LAD, UNDER THE COMMAND OF GENERAL GRANT... UNION ARMY, EIGHTEEN SIXTY-FOUR!
GOLLY!
AND YOU TWO ARE LITTLE ARCHIE AND BETTY! I'VE SEEN YOU TWO PLAYING IN THE FIELDS!
BUT IF YOU'VE SEEN US BEFORE, WHY HAVEN'T WE SEEN YOU?
BECAUSE USUALLY I'M INVISIBLE... WATCH!
POOF!
DROP AROUND TOMORROW, CHILDREN! SHOW STARTS AS SOON AS THE WRECKING CREW ARRIVES!
OKAY, MR. COLLINS!
YOU KNOW, BETTY, TOMORROW SHOULD BE A MOST INTERESTING DAY!
5

THE NEXT MORNING--
LET 'ER GO, AL! PUT THE BULLDOZER TO IT!
I-I CAN'T STEER! SOMETHING'S GOT HOLD OF MY ARM!
CRASH!
WHAT'S WRONG WITH YOU GUYS? C'MON! WE'LL START KNOCKING DOWN THE HOUSE WITH SLEDGEHAMMERS!
6

I DON'T GET IT! SOMETHING SEEMED TO GRAB-
YOU CAN'T TEAR THIS HOUSE DOWN, MISTER! THE GHOST OF GENERAL COLLINS WON'T LET YOU!
HAR! HAR! HEAR THAT, BOYS! THE KID SAYS A GHOST IS--
YIII!
MY MEN THINK THE OLD COLLINS PLACE IS HAUNTED, MR. MAYOR! THEY WON'T WORK!
HARUMPH! POPPYCOCK! I'LL BE RIGHT OVER!
MAYOR
NOW WHAT'S ALL THIS FOOLISHNESS ABOUT?
THESE MEN ARE CONVINCED THIS HOUSE IS SPOOKED, MR. MAYOR!
NONSENSE! WOULD I BE STANDING HERE IF I THOUGHT THERE WAS A GHOST AROUND?
NO, SIR!
I GUESS NOT!
7

WAP!
YOU'D BETTER GET OVER HERE, GOVERNOR! THERE SEEMS TO BE A STORY THAT A (HARUMPH) GHOST IS LIVING ON STATE HIGHWAY PROPERTY!
PSSST! I HEARD THE MAYOR TELEPHONE THE GOVERNOR TO COME OVER HERE! I'VE GOT AN IDEA THAT'LL REALLY SELL THE GOVERNOR IF YOU'LL HELP ME, LITTLE ARCHIE!
THIS BOY STARTED THE STORY, YOUR HONOR!
YES, SIR, YOU SEE, THE GHOST OF GENERAL COLLINS STILL LIVES HERE!
GENERAL COLLINS LOVES HIS OLD HOME AND REFUSES TO LET IT BE TORN DOWN!
HARUMPH! DO YOU EXPECT THE GOVERNOR TO BELIEVE A WILD TALE LIKE THAT?
GOVERNOR, IF I DID HANDSTANDS ABOVE THE ROOF OF THE HOUSE, WOULD YOU BELIEVE THE STORY ABOUT THE GHOST?
WELL, I GUESS I'D HAVE TO!
8

LET'S GO! GENERAL COLLINS!
WHEE!
HOW'S THAT, GOVERNOR?
YOU'VE CONVINCED ME! THE GHOST IS REAL!
BUT UNLESS WE CAN THINK OF A WAY TO USE THIS PROPERTY, I COULDN'T AGREE TO BUILD THE ROAD AROUND RIVERDALE!
GENERAL COLLINS HAS AN IDEA, SIR!
9

THE HOUSE IS LARGE AND IN FAIR SHAPE! WITH A LITTLE WORK YOU COULD.... BZZZZZ
SPLENDID!
B-BUT THE HIGH-WAY!
ELECTIONS ARE COMING UP, MAYOR! THESE MEN ARE VOTERS!
ULP!
I NEED NOT REMIND YOU MEN THAT IF THIS STORY LEAKS OUT, WE'LL ALL BE LOCKED UP IN PADDED CELLS!
A FEW WEEKS LATER-
THE HIGHWAY ROUTE IS CHANGED! THE COLLINS PLACE IS FIXED UP! WONDER WHAT MADE THE GOVERNOR CHANGE HIS MIND?
MAYBE SOMETHING CAME TO HIM OUT OF THIN AIR!
STILL, I BET THE OLD GENERAL WOULD REALLY FLIP IF HE KNEW HIS HOUSE IS FILLED WITH CHILDREN NOW!
NOPE! I'D SAY HE'S PRETTY HAPPY!
STATE ORPHANAGE
ORPHANAGE ENTRANCE
THE END
10

Archie
IN
VIDIOCY
RONNIE'S NEW INSTANT TV PLAYBACK CAMERA IS FANTASTIC!
I AGREE! HERE'S A VIDEO TAPE I TOOK OF YOU JUST SECONDS AGO ON THE PATIO!
SMACK! SMACK!
RONNIE'S NEW INSTANT TV PLAYBACK CAMERA IS FOR THE BIRDS!
END

Archie
IN
DISTAFF GAFF
ARCHIE, YOUR SAUCE IS MUCH TOO THIN!
WELL, WHAT DO YOU EXPECT FROM A BOY?
COOKING ASSIGNMENT Pg.22
BUT WHAT DO YOU THINK OF MY CAKE?
FOR A BOY, IT ISN'T BAD!
WHAT DID YOU LEARN IN SCHOOL TODAY, SON?
R
THAT THE WORLD IS FULL OF FEMALE CHAUVINISTS!
R
END

Archie
-in-
"FLOWER POWER"
AHH! I WONDERED WHERE YOU DISAPPEARED TO!
YOU WERE PUSHED BEHIND ALL MY OTHER BOOKS!
A CRUSHED DAISY! BOY! YOU SURE BRING BACK MEMORIES!
THAT DAISY TAKES ME BACK TO THE FIRST DAY I CAME TO RIVERDALE! IT STARTED WHEN DADDY SAID...

WHAT DID YOU SAY, DADDY?
I SAID WE'RE MOVING TO A TOWN CALLED RIVERDALE!
THE BOARD HAS VOTED TO SET UP THE COMPANY'S CORPORATION HEADQUARTERS THERE!
I'LL BET THIS RIVERDALE IS NOT EVEN ON THE MAP! IT SOUNDS LIKE A HICK TOWN!
I'M NOT GOING, AND YOU'RE NOT GOING TO MAKE ME!
ALL OUT FOR RIVERDALE!
OH, GOODY! THIS TOWN ACTUALLY HAS A TRAIN STATION! WOW!
COME ON, VERONICA! YOU'LL LIKE IT ONCE WE GET SETTLED! THIS IS ONLY THE FIRST DAY!
RIVERDALE
2

I MUST ADMIT OUR HOUSE IS AS BIG AS A FOOTBALL FIELD... BUT I'D LIKE TO SEE WHAT THIS TOWN LOOKS LIKE!

VERY QUAINT... IT LOOKS LIKE A PICTURE POSTCARD!

?

I GET A FUNNY FEELING...

SOMEONE IS...

... FOLLOWING ME!
3

MMM... I WONDER WHAT ICE CREAM TASTES LIKE IN THIS SMALL TOWN...
PO

ONE POP TATE SPECIAL FOR THE YOUNG LADY WHO JUST MOVED INTO TOWN!

GULP! HOW DID YOU KNOW?

THIS IS A SMALL TOWN... BUT NEWS GETS AROUND FAST! EVERYBODY KNOWS EVERYBODY!
OH?

ER... WHO IS THAT BOY WHO NEVER TURNS OFF THAT SILLY ONE-HUNDRED WATT SMILE... AND KEEPS FOLLOWING ME?

OH, THAT'S ARCHIE ANDREWS!
ARCHIE ANDREWS, EH?
4

STOP FOLLOWING ME .!!!
I'LL GIVE YOU TILL TEN TO GET OUT OF MY SIGHT!
...AND I'M COUNTING BY FIVES!
ZIP!
GULP! HE REALLY DID GO! I DIDN'T THINK I WAS THAT ... GOOD!
GEE! I WALKED HOME AND I DIDN'T SEE 'WHAT'S-HIS-NAME' ONCE! JUST WHEN I WAS BEGINNING TO THINK HE WAS CUTE!
RING!
HI, I SHOULD HAVE INTRODUCED MYSELF... FORMALLY! MY NAME IS ARCHIE ANDREWS, AND I WOULD LIKE TO WELCOME YOU TO...
5

SLAM!
SOMETIMES I'M TOO HASTY! THAT WAS A SWEET THING FOR THAT SMALL TOWN KID TO DO...
YES! I THINK I MIGHT JUST GET TO LIKE THIS TOWN CALLED RIVERDALE... AND EVEN THAT ARCHIE!
HI, VERONICA! THOUGHT WE COULD GO FOR A SODA!
KISS!
YOU DON'T HAVE TO THANK ME FOR A SODA!
NO! FOR A DAISY!
END

Archie
IN
"AIL TALE"
ARCH, HOW COME YOU DIDN'T GO TO SCHOOL TODAY?
I FELT SICK!
THE ENTIRE SCHOOL WENT TO A MAJOR LEAGUE BALL GAME TODAY!
NOW I REALLY DO FEEL SICK!
END
Betty
IN
PRIME TIME
ETHEL DID THE MILE IN 6:02!
WHAT'S YOUR BEST TIME, BETTY?
SIGH! THE TIME I SPEND WITH ARCHIE!
END

Archie in BONE ZONE
DIG THE DIFFERENT SYMBOLS THE COACH PUT ON OUR WARM-UP JACKETS!
WHY THE TIGER?
BECAUSE I PLAY LIKE ONE!
D-UH.! HE PUT A STAR ON MINE BECAUSE I AM A STAR!
AND WHAT DOES YOUR SYMBOL STAND FOR, ARCHIE?
I DUNNO! I'LL ASK!
HEY, COACH!
WHAT IS IT, BONEHEAD ANDREWS?
END

Archie
in
"INQUIRY"
HI, MOOSE!
HI, ARCH!
HOW ARE YOU FEELING?
JUST FINE, AND YOU?
COULDN'T BE BETTER!
THAT'S GOOD!
SLAP!
WELL, ON SECOND THOUGHT!
The End!

Betty and Veronica in "BIG CHEER"
SATURDAY
WOW! I CAN'T BELIEVE OUR SQUAD JUST WON THE REGIONALS!
THERE'S SOMETHING ELSE I CAN'T BELIEVE...
REGIONAL CHEERLEADING CHAMPIONSHIP
...HARDLY ANYONE SHOWED UP TO CHEER US CHEERLEADERS!
WHAT'S MORE, NO ONE FROM OUR FOOTBALL TEAM WAS HERE!
AND AFTER ALL THE SUPPORT WE'VE GIVEN THOSE GUYS!

MONDAY FOOTBALL PRACTICE...
LOOKEE! HERE COME THE GIRLS!
NO DOUBT TO TELL US HOW MUCH THEY ENJOY BEING ABLE TO CHEER US TO VICTORY!
OUR SQUAD WON THE REGIONALS LAST WEEK!
AND NOT ONE OF YOU DUDES WAS THERE TO ENCOURAGE US!
WE ENJOY CHEERING FOR THE FOOTBALL TEAM...
BUT THIS HAS TO BE A TWO WAY STREET! GET WITH IT!
GEE! WHAT'S GOTTEN INTO BETTY AND VERONICA?
I THINK THEY BACK FLIPPED ONCE TOO OFTEN!
THEY HAVE NO IDEA HOW BUSY WE ARE JUST PLAYING FOOTBALL!
YEAH! THAT'S FOR SURE!
2

I STILL CAN'T GET OVER THE GIRLS COMING DOWN ON US!
MAYBE EXAM WEEK HAS THEM ON EDGE!
GEE, ALICIA! WHAT'S WITH YOUR ARM?
SHE INJURED IT DOING A TRICKY CHEER-LEADER STUNT!
IT'S NOT TOO BAD! THE DOC SAYS I SHOULD BE ABLE TO REJOIN THE SQUAD NEXT YEAR!
NEXT YEAR?
DIG THE BIG LINEUP OF GIRLS!
I WONDER WHAT IT'S ALL ABOUT?
WE'RE ALL COMPETING TO SEE WHO REPLACES ALICIA ON THE SQUAD!
CHEERLEADER TRYOUTS TODAY
ALL OF YOU JUST FOR ONE OPENING?
THAT'S NOT SURPRISING! THE COMPETITION TO BE A CHEERLEADER IS SOMETHING FIERCE!
3

ALL THE GIRLS ON THE SQUAD HAVE TO BE ABLE TO DO THE SPLITS!
IT'S TAKEN ME MONTHS TO GET IT DOWN!
I HEAR THE GIRL WHO MAKES THE SQUAD WILL HAVE TO PRACTICE THREE HOURS A DAY!
I SHOULD BE SO LUCKY!
CHEERLEADER TRYOUTS TODAY
GEE! I HAD NO IDEA THE CHEER-LEADERS WORKED SO HARD!
NEITHER DID I, CHUCK!
GYMNASIUM
LOOK! I'VE AN IDEA... BZZ.. BZZ BZZZ...
SOUNDS PRETTY COOL TO ME!
FRIDAY NIGHT...
THAT WAS THE LAST PLAY OF THE HALF!
RIVERDALE AND OCEANSIDE ARE STILL LOCKED IN A 7-7 TIE!
SOMETHING IS GOING ON...
THE RIVERDALE PLAYERS ARE NOT LEAVING THE FIELD!

BEFORE EVERYONE STARTS STREAKING FOR THE HOT DOG STAND, THE GUYS AND I WOULD LIKE TO SAY A FEW WORDS!
?
!
?
!
ANDREWS
17
12
R
NEXT WEEK OUR GIRLS ARE COMPETING FOR THE COUNTY CHEERLEADING CHAMPIONSHIP!
LET'S ALL SHOW UP TO CHEER THE CHEERLEADERS!
12
17
22
...AND NOW WE'D LIKE TO LEAVE YOU ALL WITH A MESSAGE THAT'S LONG OVERDUE!
TWO... FOUR... SIX... EIGHT! WHO DO WE APPRECIATE? OUR CHEERLEADERS! OUR CHEERLEADERS!
OUR BOYS MAY BE ONLY # 5 IN THE LEAGUE, BUT # 1 IN OUR HEARTS!
12
17
24
10
END

ARCHIE...
YES, MR. MORGANSTERN!
SUPER SOUP SALE
12
2 for 99
14
SOUP
WOBBLE
WOBBLE
SOUP
Archie
in
"GETTING CANNED"
W-WH-WHOAAA!
SOUP
I KNEW IT! I KNEW IT!
CRASH!
CLANG
CLANK
MGR

ARCHIE, YOU OKAY?
I'M FINE, SIR! WHAT DID YOU WANT?
I WAS GOING TO TELL YOU TO BE CAREFUL!
OH... RIGHT! SHOULD I STACK THOSE CANS AGAIN, SIR?
NO! NO! I'LL GET MATT TO DO THAT! GO UP FRONT AND HELP WITH CHECK-OUT!
YES, SIR!
TODAY IS ONE OF THOSE DAYS WHEN ARCHIE JUST CAN'T DO ANYTHING RIGHT!
A BIT LATER...
THERE YOU ARE, MRS. SNYDER!
THANK YOU, ARCHIE! BUT I HOPE YOU DIDN'T OVERPACK THE BAGS!
1 2 3
SALE
MGR
SALE
2

THOSE BAGS DO LOOK A LITTLE HEAVY, ARCHIE!
HERE, LET ME GET THEM!
3
OOF! THERE! NOW INTO THE CART AND...
OH, NO! NOT AGAIN!
YIPE!!
OH, MY GOSH!
RIPPP!
BANG
KLANK
KLUNK
KLUNK
AFTER THINGS ARE COLLECTED...
PUSH THIS OUT TO MRS. SNYDER'S CAR, ARCHIE! THEN COLLECT THE CARTS IN THE LOT!
RIGHT-O, SIR!
COLLECTING CARTS SHOULD KEEP HIM OUT OF TROUBLE!
SALE 2 FOR 99¢
3

MINUTES LATER...
HUMPH! COLLECTING CARTS ISN'T MUCH FUN!
THANKS, ARCHIE! HAVE FUN COLLECTING CARTS!
2120
HEY! MAYBE I CAN MAKE THIS FUN ON THE RUN!
ZIP
ANDREWS IN HIS SOUPED-UP GO-CART TAKES THE EARLY LEAD!
SUPER MARKET
ZOOM
WHOA! HE CRASHES ON THE FAR TURN!
BUMP!
WHAP!
BUT HE'S PICKING UP CARTS AND SPEED AGAIN!
WHAP
WHAP
BUMP
NOW HE'S REALLY ROLLING IN THE SUPERMARKET 500!
ZIP!
HOP
4

I WONDER WHAT'S TAKING ARCHIE SO LONG?
SALE
HUH?
YEOW! LOOK OUT! I CAN'T STEER!!
RUMBLE RUMBLE
YIKES! ARCHIE! STOP!
I- I'M TRYING TO, SIR!
SOUP
RUMBLE
RUMBLE
SCREECH
UH-OH!
SODA
POP!
SHOPPING CART STAMPEDE!
HELP!
KARASH!
MGR
5

GET ME OUT OF HERE!!
I'M COMING, SIR!
GULP! A-AM I CANNED, SIR?
NO! BUT I HAVE A SPECIAL JOB FOR YOU UNTIL YOUR SHIFT IS OVER!
A SPECIAL JOB? WHAT, SIR?
FOR THE REST OF TODAY YOU'RE A SAFETY SPOT CHECKER!
21
22
SHAMPOO 2.95
2 FOR 99
MGR
LATER...
YOU MEAN ALL I DO IS SIT HERE AND HAND OUT COUPONS FOR THE REST OF MY SHIFT?
THAT'S RIGHT!
BUT HOW DOES THAT MAKE ME A SAFETY SPOT CHECKER?
AS LONG AS YOU STAY IN THE ONE SPOT, EVERYONE ELSE IS SAFE!
FREE COUPONS

LISTEN UP, SLICK TOP, AND LISTEN UP GOOD!! YOU TANGLE WITH ME AND YOU'RE HISTORY! I AM THE GREATEST!!
GEE, ARCHIE, WHAT ARE YOU GETTING SO MAD ABOUT? CALM DOWN! LET'S TALK THIS OVER!
RIVERDA PARK
* NO! THERE'S NO MISTAKE! THE BALLOONS ARE WHERE THEY'RE SUPPOSED TO BE! ... BUT IT SEEMS KINDA BACKWARD, DOESN'T IT?
Archie
-in-
"SWITCH HITTER"
HERE'S HOW IT ALL CAME ABOUT...
HI, REG! I HEAR YOU HAVE A GUEST AT YOUR HOUSE!
RIGHT, ARCH!
R
MY UNCLE CODY, FROM HOLLYWOOD!
CODY! THAT'S AN UNUSUAL NAME!
1

IT WAS HORACE WHEN HE WAS BORN ... BUT YOU KNOW THOSE MOVIE PEOPLE!
"MOVIE"?
HE'S ONE OF THOSE MAKE-UP ARTISTS! HE PERFORMS MIRACLES!
COME OFF IT, REG! STOP EXAGGERATING!
FOLLOW ME, SKEPTIC! YOU GOTTA MEET MY UNCLE!
SURE! I HAVEN'T SEEN A MIRACLE IN DAYS!
HYUK!
UNCLE CODY! THIS IS ARCHIE! HE DOESN'T BELIEVE WHAT YOU CAN DO WITH YOUR MAKE-UP KIT!
HMM! I LOVE A CHALLENGE!
LET'S SEE! I THINK I HAVE A WIG IN JUST THAT SHADE!
?
WHAT ARE YOU GONNA DO?
HOLD STILL! I'M TURNING YOU INTO TWINS! LEMME GET THESE FRECKLES ON!
YIPE! YOU'RE GONNA MAKE ME LOOK LIKE HIM? SOME UNCLE YOU ARE!
2

WOW! THAT'S AMAZING!
GOOD GRIEF! TWO ARCHIES IN THE SAME TOWN?
KNOW WHAT'D BE A GAS?-- MAKIN' HIM LOOK LIKE ME!!
HMM! LET ME CHECK MY WIGS, REGGIE!
NOT BAD! IF YOU CAN MAKE THAT NASTY LITTLE SNEER OF REGGIE'S!
GLEEP! DO I GOTTA?
SHOOT! YOU GOT THE BETTER OF THE DEAL, ARCH! YOU LOOK LIKE ME!
THIS IS A HOOT! COME ON, LET'S GO FOOL SOMEBODY!
HI, JUG, OL' PAL! HOW'RE THINGS?
WHAT DO YOU CARE, YOU CREEP? DON'T TRY THAT "MR. NICE GUY" ON ME!!
3

LOOK! IT'S ME! ARCHIE! REGGIE'S UNCLE IS A HOLLYWOOD MAKE-UP MAN! IS HE A GENIUS, OR WHAT?!
REGGIE GOT THE BETTER OF IT, ARCH! HE LOOKS LIKE YOU!
YOU GUYS KEEP YAKKING! THERE'S SOMEONE I WANT TO SEE, ALONE!
DON'T DO ANYTHING I WOULDN'T DO, REG!
WELL, AREN'T YOU THE LUCKY LADY? LOOK WHAT GOOD FORTUNE SMILES ON YOU TODAY!
ARCHIE? YOU, TOOTING YOUR OWN HORN? HOW UNLIKE YOU!
LODGE
RIGHT! I DECIDED TO DROP THE DORKY ROUTINE AND SMARTEN UP!
YOU WERE NEVER A DORK, ARCHIE! A LITTLE ON THE NERD SIDE, BUT NEVER A DORK!
WELL, AREN'T YOU GOING TO PUCKER UP AND KISS AWAY MY NERDINESS, YOU FORTUNATE FEMALE?
HEY! A LITTLE NERDINESS IS NOT NECESSARILY A BAD THING, YOU CONCEITED CREEP!!
4

HEY, NO PAIN, NO GAIN! I GOT WHAT I WANTED! I TURNED HER OFF OL' ARCH!
THIS IS TOO GOOD TO WASTE! NOW TO SEE IF I CAN TURN BETTY OFF MR. WONDERFUL!
BETTY COOPER, HOW IN THE WORLD DO YOU DO IT?
DO WHAT, ARCHIE?
GET MORE BEAUTIFUL EVERY DAY! WHY, PRETTY SOON, YOU'LL BE WORTHY OF--ME!!
HUH? ARCHIE! WHAT'S GOT INTO YOU?
JUST POINTING OUT, SWEET LIPS, THAT YOU'LL BE ABLE TO DATE THE CREAM OF THE CROP! ...AND THAT, OF COURSE, IS GOOD OL'-R-R... ARCHIE!!
THIS IS REVOLTING, ARCHIE!
YOU'RE BEGINNING TO SOUND LIKE A CERTAIN UNMENTIONABLE CHARACTER, WHOM I DON'T CARE TO MENTION! SEE ME WHEN YOUR HEAD GETS BACK TO NORMAL SIZE!
5

SO WHO DID YOU HAVE TO GO SEE, REG?
BETTY AND VERONICA! I LEFT THEM WITH AN IMPRESSION OF YOU THAT YOU WOULDN'T BELIEVE!
THAT'S IT! I KNEW YOU'D PULL SOME NASTY TRICK! I'M THROUGH WITH THIS MASQUERADE!
FINE! I'M SICK OF LOOKIN' LIKE A DORK!!
WHAP!
PLOP!
YOU, TOO? WHATEVER GOT INTO HIM?
PATTED HIMSELF ON THE BACK SO HARD, I THOUGHT HE'D BREAK HIS ARM!
HOWDY DOODY, GIRLS! SEEN OUR OL' BUDDY ARCH LATELY?
YOU STAY AWAY FROM ARCHIE, YOU CREEP!!
YOU'VE CONTAMINATED THE POOR BOY! HE'S BEGINNING TO SOUND MORE LIKE YOU EVERY DAY!
-AND THE LAST THING THIS TOWN NEEDS IS TWO REGGIE MANTLES!!
?
SPLASH!
The End